T0131813

God's
Great Garden
Ten Terrific Gifts God Created for You!

Suzanne A. Fischer

AuthorHouse™
1663 Liberty Drive
Bloomington, IN 47403
www.authorhouse.com
Phone: 1 (800) 839-8640

© 2018 Suzanne A. Fischer. All rights reserved.

No part of this book may be reproduced, stored in a retrieval system,
or transmitted by any means without the written permission of the author.

Published by AuthorHouse 10/11/2018

ISBN: 978-1-5462-4054-9 (sc)
ISBN: 978-1-5462-4055-6 (e)

Library of Congress Control Number: 2018912048

Print information available on the last page.

Any people depicted in stock imagery provided by Getty Images are models,
and such images are being used for illustrative purposes only.
Certain stock imagery © Getty Images.

This book is printed on acid-free paper.

Because of the dynamic nature of the Internet, any web addresses or links contained in this
book may have changed since publication and may no longer be valid. The views expressed
in this work are solely those of the author and do not necessarily reflect the views of
the publisher, and the publisher hereby disclaims any responsibility for them.

authorHOUSE®

"God's Great Garden is a wonderful and engaging story that families can share together. My name is Mirelle Robello. I am a Kindergarten teacher for Pinellas County Schools in Florida. I know my students would love this book and I am eager to add it to my classroom library. I truly enjoyed reading God's Great Garden and look forward to sharing with my co-workers and present and future students."

Mirelle Robello

When I was little, I was outside...... in the woods, the garden, or exploring somewhere I "didn't belong."

I like that in a few short minutes, I became excited, once again, by the great variety and diversity in nature.

Kim Schotte, Horse Farm owner, nature lover.

"My connection to Suzi Fischer has spanned more than thirty eight years. In the early years, I knew her as an amazing kindergarten teacher who loved watching the bright eyes of small children as they would learn. She had a very child-centered classroom that focused on the individual student and it was both nurturing and academic. Suzi provided opportunities for her students to learn through experiences. She worked to help them develop thought processes and skills in speaking and listening. Suzi knew that children's literature was a way to create excitement for learning. She could make a book come alive, and her passion for reading became her students' passion.

Later, I knew Suzi as a curriculum specialist in the school where I was the assistant principal. She wanted to have a greater impact on a larger number of students, and she knew that this could be accomplished by mentoring teachers. Her expertise was held in high regard as she guided teachers through the curriculum, teaching practices and climate of the classroom. She monitored student learning, and routinely assisted teachers with ideas to foster a love of reading in their students. Suzi was well suited for this role, for helping others has always been a spiritual focus for her life."

Karen Moseley, parent, School Principal (retired)

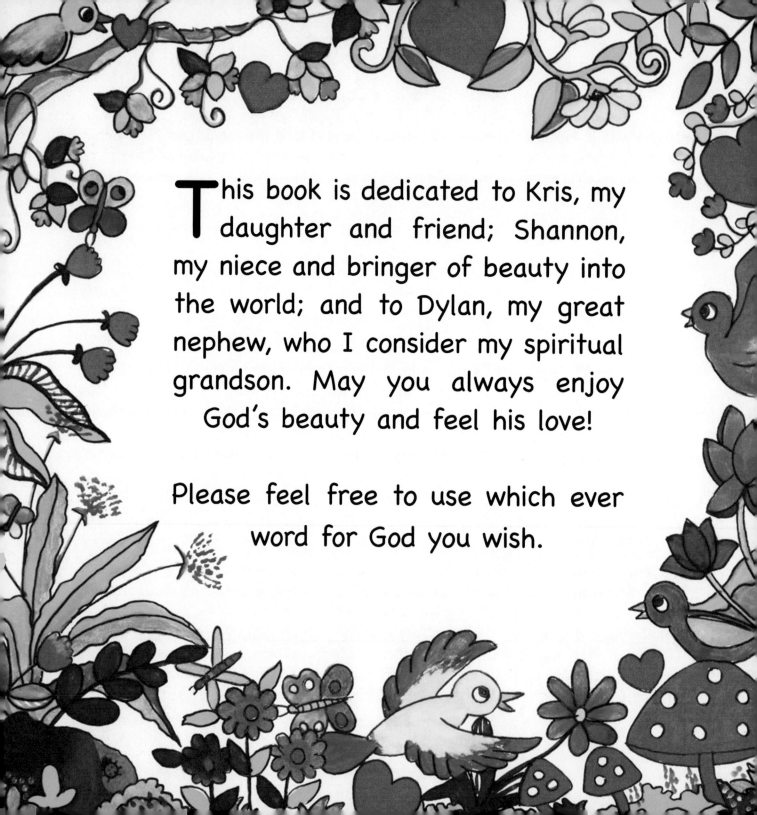

This book is dedicated to Kris, my daughter and friend; Shannon, my niece and bringer of beauty into the world; and to Dylan, my great nephew, who I consider my spiritual grandson. May you always enjoy God's beauty and feel his love!

Please feel free to use which ever word for God you wish.

Ten Terrific Gifts God Created for you

Flowers
Birds
Bugs
Snowflakes
Sun
Stars
Gems and Stones
Music
Voices
Variety and Diversity

"God saw all that He had made, and it was very good."
Genesis 1:31

One afternoon, Angel was visiting her
aunt and went outside to play in Aunt
Suzi's garden. She sat on a bench and
noticed a pretty flower. Angel picked
it and smelled it. It smelled so good!

She wondered to herself, "Why is it, God, that there are so many different flowers? They come in so many different sizes, shapes, colors, and scents."

Suddenly, the wind blew and a beautiful light swirled around her. She felt very excited! God answered her. She could hear His voice in her heart.

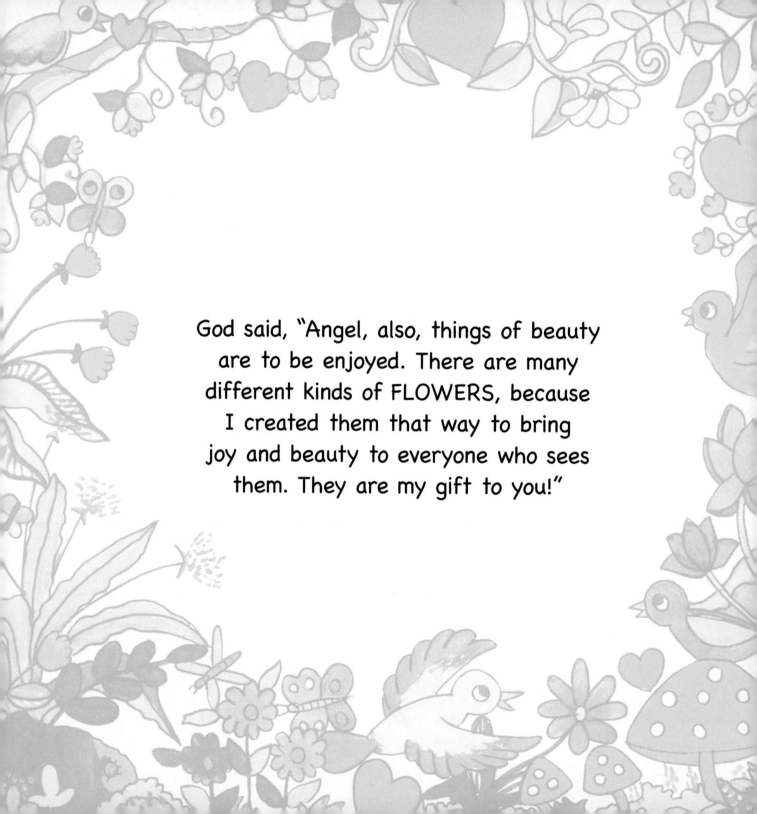

God said, "Angel, also, things of beauty
are to be enjoyed. There are many
different kinds of FLOWERS, because
I created them that way to bring
joy and beauty to everyone who sees
them. They are my gift to you!"

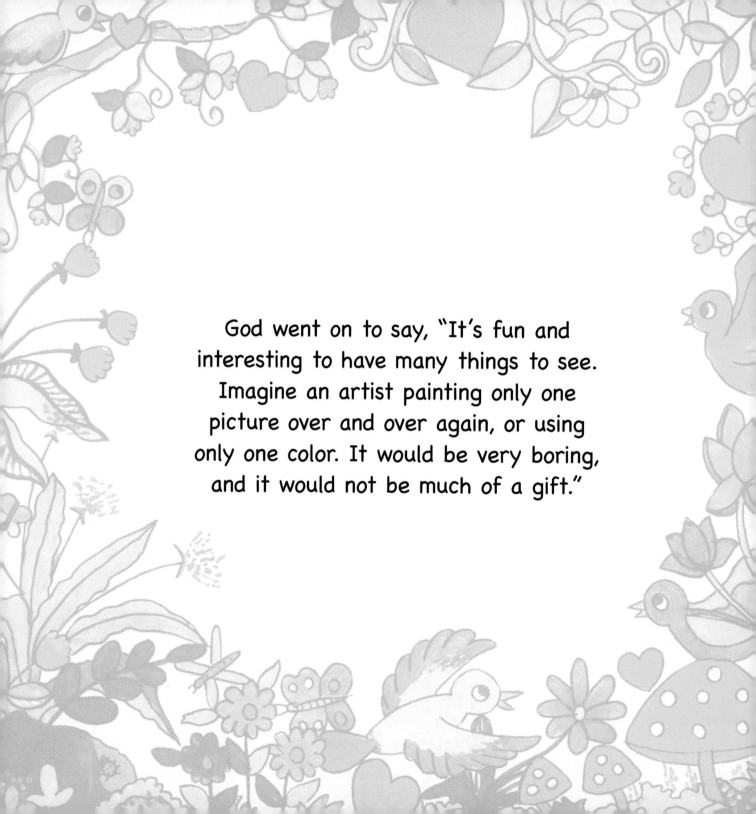

God went on to say, "It's fun and interesting to have many things to see. Imagine an artist painting only one picture over and over again, or using only one color. It would be very boring, and it would not be much of a gift."

Just then, Angel saw a bird eat a
bug and then zoom away. "Yuck!" she
thought. "What do bugs taste like?"
she wondered. "What about the birds
and the bugs?" Angel asked God as
she buzzed around the garden.

"BIRDS are another gift. Birds and other
animals also come in many different
varieties," He answered. "There are birds
that eat bugs, birds that eat seeds,
and even birds that eat mice and other
small animals. Some birds are blue, some
are red, and some have many colors,
like parrots. They don't need to come
in so many shapes, sizes, and colors.
It is just more lovely that way."

"BUGS are really fun!

There are creepy, crawly bugs;
flying, buzzing bugs; hopping
bugs, and climbing bugs.

There are tiny bugs, big bugs,
and middle-sized bugs.

Some bugs sting or bite, while other bugs
are fun to play with, like the Ladybug.

Do you know that there are over 40,000
different species of just spiders?"

"Wow!" Angel said as she listened
closely to every word, sitting
back down on the bench.

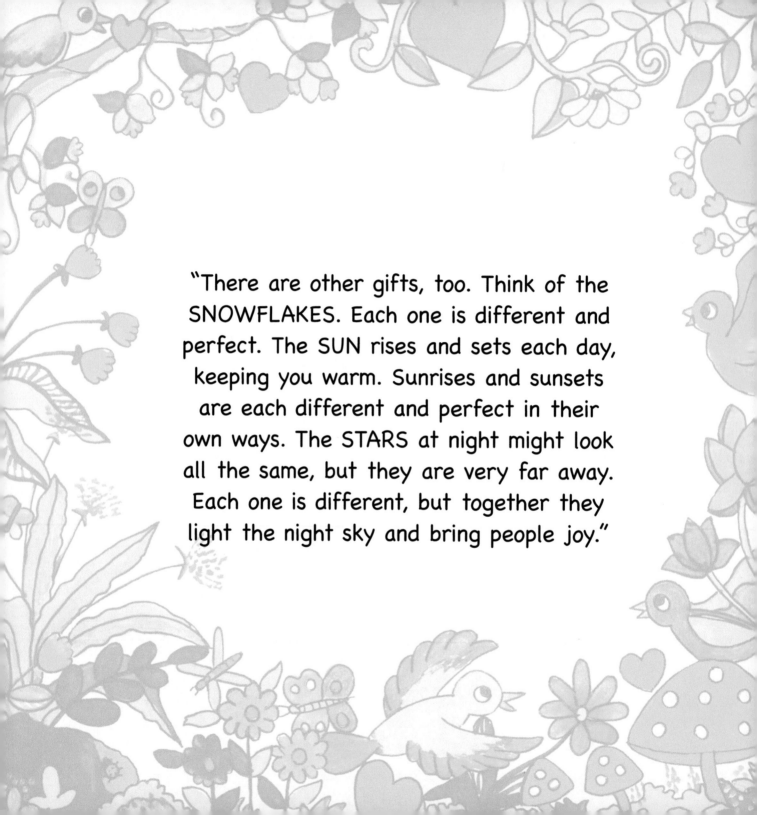

"There are other gifts, too. Think of the SNOWFLAKES. Each one is different and perfect. The SUN rises and sets each day, keeping you warm. Sunrises and sunsets are each different and perfect in their own ways. The STARS at night might look all the same, but they are very far away. Each one is different, but together they light the night sky and bring people joy."

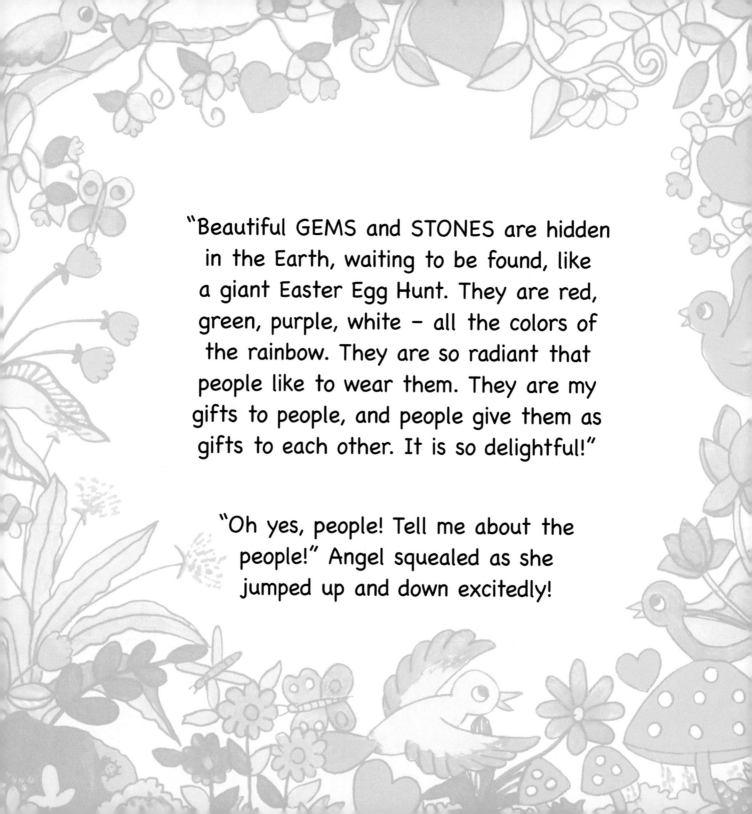

"Beautiful GEMS and STONES are hidden in the Earth, waiting to be found, like a giant Easter Egg Hunt. They are red, green, purple, white – all the colors of the rainbow. They are so radiant that people like to wear them. They are my gifts to people, and people give them as gifts to each other. It is so delightful!"

"Oh yes, people! Tell me about the people!" Angel squealed as she jumped up and down excitedly!

"Once again, there is a great amount of VARIETY and DIVERSITY among people. In some ways people are all the same. They are all children of God, but have different skin colors, eye colors, and hair colors. People also come in all shapes and sizes."

"Look closely and you will see that even ears and noses are different. If all people looked the same, how on Earth would you ever find your mother and father? People also have different voices and fingerprints. These prints are so individual that people can be identified by their voiceprints or their fingerprints. That, to me, is one of my finest achievements!"

"I like to sing with my voice, and I like to hear music" Angel responded, singing "La, la, la" to herself.

"VOICES, beautiful voices are music to my ears. Voices for speaking, playing, laughing, teaching, singing, and praying – I love them all. Voices can be high or low, loud or soft, or somewhere in between. When they all come together in a choir to make a joyful sound for me, I am thrilled! Having a voice to talk and sing with is a very great gift."

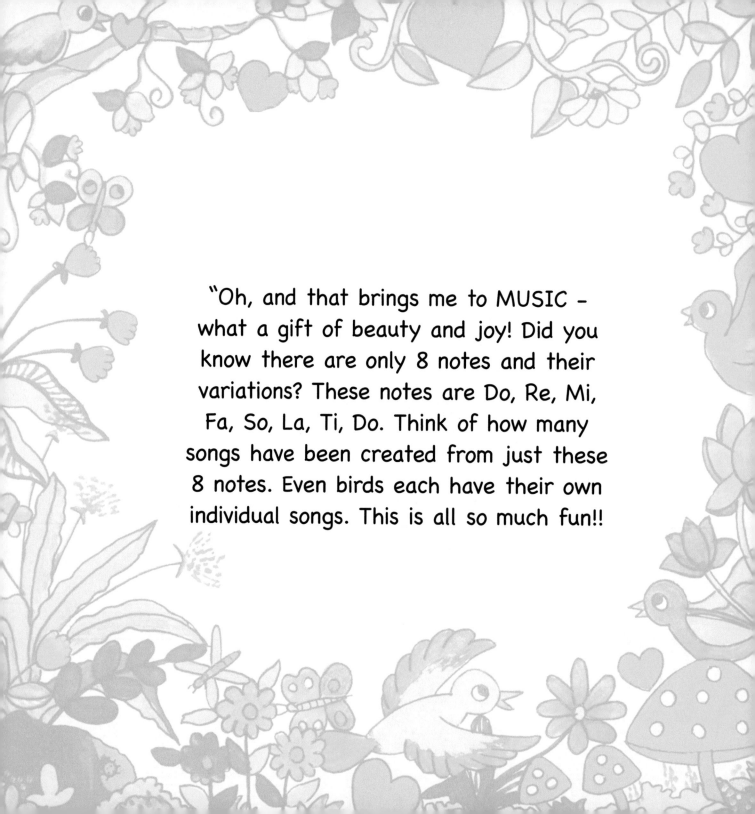

"Oh, and that brings me to MUSIC –
what a gift of beauty and joy! Did you
know there are only 8 notes and their
variations? These notes are Do, Re, Mi,
Fa, So, La, Ti, Do. Think of how many
songs have been created from just these
8 notes. Even birds each have their own
individual songs. This is all so much fun!!

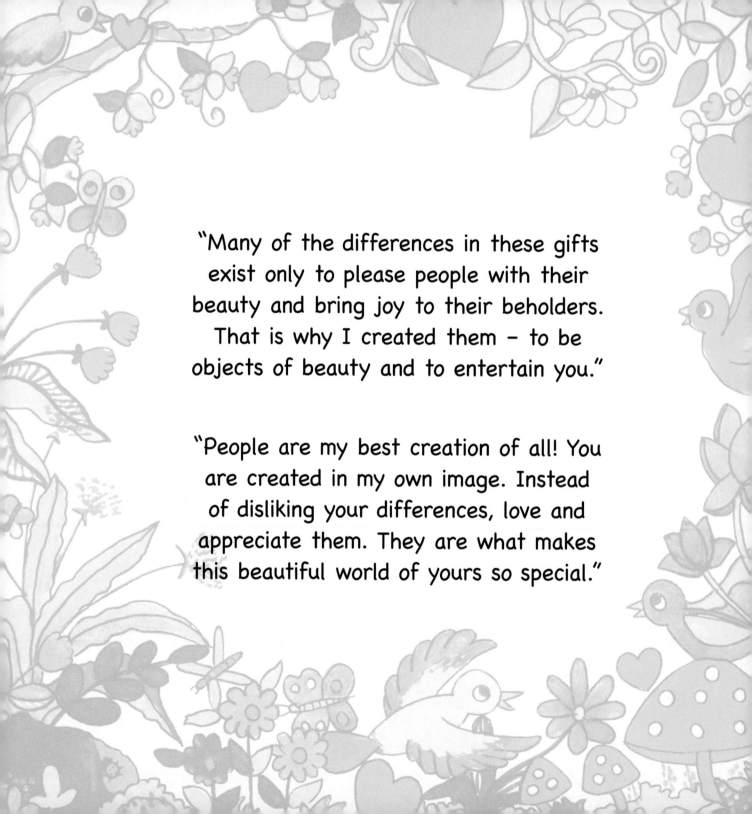

"Many of the differences in these gifts exist only to please people with their beauty and bring joy to their beholders. That is why I created them – to be objects of beauty and to entertain you."

"People are my best creation of all! You are created in my own image. Instead of disliking your differences, love and appreciate them. They are what makes this beautiful world of yours so special."

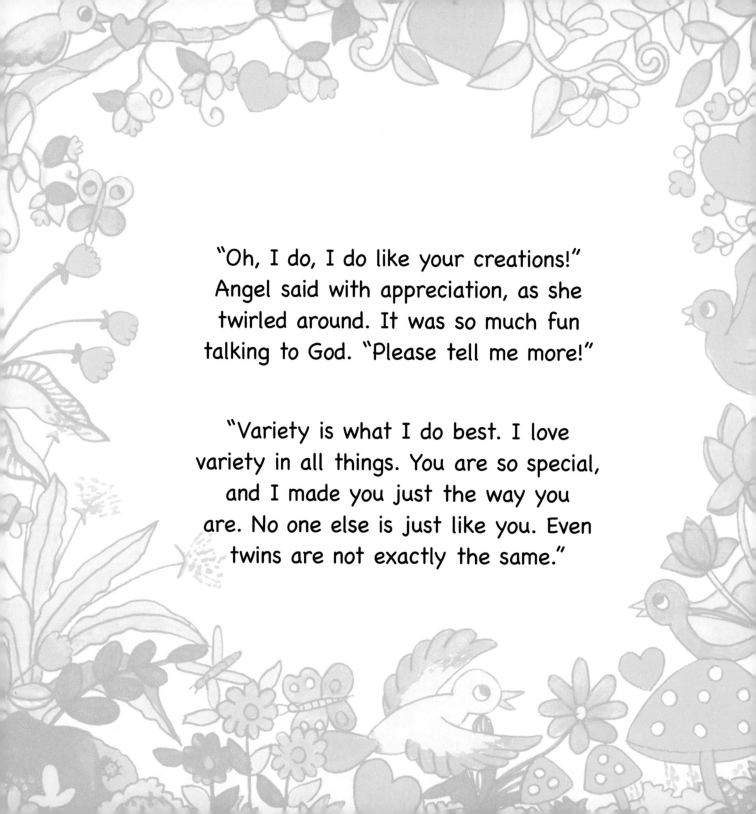

"Oh, I do, I do like your creations!" Angel said with appreciation, as she twirled around. It was so much fun talking to God. "Please tell me more!"

"Variety is what I do best. I love variety in all things. You are so special, and I made you just the way you are. No one else is just like you. Even twins are not exactly the same."

"I created all things, gave all things, and all things are loved by me. All things are perfect. There are no mistakes. All things have purpose and beauty. All, in my eyes, are beautiful."

"Do I have a purpose, too?" Angel asked, swinging her legs back and forth.

"Yes, Angel, and you shall discover it someday. You will do the things you came here to do."

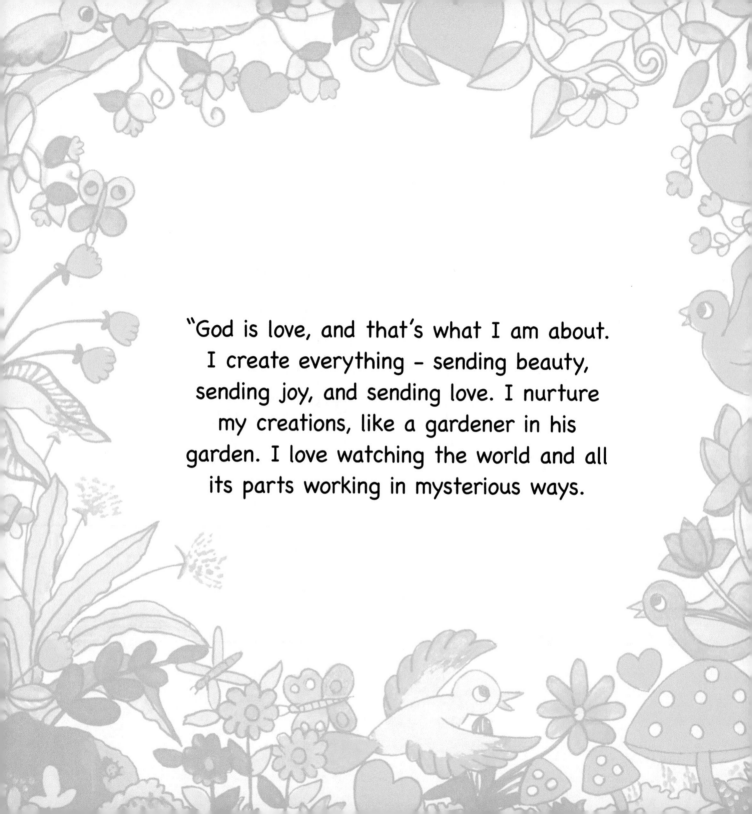

"God is love, and that's what I am about. I create everything – sending beauty, sending joy, and sending love. I nurture my creations, like a gardener in his garden. I love watching the world and all its parts working in mysterious ways.

When He finished, Angel was tired and everything was quiet. She found herself lying down on the bench. Angel looked around the garden and saw all the flowers, birds, and bugs. Everything she could see was looking back at her and sparkling brightly. Angel saw them with new eyes, new wonder, and new love.

Angel said to God, "Oh thank you, thank you, thank you for sending me all these terrific gifts. I will love all of them, just like you love me!!"

All things bright and beautiful,
All creatures great and small,
All things wise and wonderful,
The Lord God made them all.

Here are some Web site links to two versions of "All things
Bright and Beautiful" for you and your children to enjoy.

http://www.youtube.com/watch?v=eLeq2vj9kcA

http://www.youtube.com/
watch?v=mRHsTA0tGEk&NR=1&feature=fvwp

Dear Grownups,

Throughout my life, I have wondered about and enjoyed God's amazing creations. At some point in time, early man's mental evolution got to the point where he began to appreciate the beauty of things and to derive joy from them. It is not known for sure, but humans seem to be the only animals capable of appreciating beauty. This is a special gift that we should all be taking time to enjoy!

The more I wondered about and appreciated these things, the more ideas came to me. I was suddenly at that crucial point where I thought, "Maybe I should write a book!" So I started to write down all of the creations I could think of. There were so many, I didn't know where to stop.

It is my hope that this book will find its way to mothers, aunts, grandmothers, and other adults, and that it will be a beginning way to start taking time to notice all of the beauty in the world.

I heard a new term awhile back – "nature deficit." It means that our children do not get out into nature enough. You can make sure this does not happen to your children. Fill their lives with nature and exploration. Go to gardens, parks, zoos, and forests. Explore how things are alike and different: compare and contrast. This is an important skill in schools today.

Compare people in your family, and other people, see how they are alike and different. Teach your children to appreciate our differences. This is a good time to talk about bullying and how it is not nice to make fun of other people for being different. Teach your children that God made them and all others perfect just the way they are!

Concepts in this book include: • appreciation • art/artist • beauty • body parts • colors • comparison • contrast • creation • design • differences • diversity • Earth • enjoyment • exploration • fragrance • fun • God • growth • happiness • imagination • individual • interest/interesting • joy • kindness • likenesses • love • music • mysterious • night/day • nurture • observation • perfect • purpose • quiet • radiant • senses • size • shape • thinking • truth • understanding • unique • variety • voices • wonder • excitement • you, yours • zoom

I could go on and on with ideas, but the point is just to enjoy your children and appreciate all of God's terrific gifts. Please feel free to use which ever word for God you wish. With love and blessings to you and yours, Suzanne Fischer, parent, teacher, author, and believer.

About the Author

Suzanne A. Fischer (BA and MA from University of South Florida), is a retired elementary school teacher, who taught Kindergarten, 1st, 3rd, 4th, and 6th grades during her 30 years of teaching. She was always partial to Kindergarten, as she found their curiosity and enthusiasm exciting. In later years, she was a Curriculum Specialist, working with children, teachers, and parents to the betterment of student education.

During her teaching years, Suzanne constantly saw a need for certain books that did not exist and always planned to write children's books during her retirement years. After retirement, Suzanne studied writing with the Institute of Children's Literature, Janet Conner (*Writing Down Your Soul)*, and the Hay House Writer's Workshop. This book is the fruition of one of those dreams.

Suzanne has always been a spiritual person, having moved into a house at age four that contained a friendly spirit. She has studied spiritual topics all of her life through books, workshops, and spiritual retreats. It is this spirituality Suzanne brings to her writing, often feeling that her work is "divinely inspired." It is for the love of God that Suzanne wishes to get her messages out into the world for others to benefit from and enjoy.

Suzanne is widowed after 38 years of marriage. She attends church regularly and sings in the choir. She has a grown daughter, who is her main proofreader and support. She raised a great niece, who she considers to be her "spiritual daughter." They all live in St. Petersburg, Florida. Her dog, Emma, keeps her company!

Special thanks goes to Linda Dillon, my spiritual advisor and friend, who kept urging me to keep working on this book.

You can contact her at: jfischer43@icloud.com

About the Illustrator

Jayamini Attanayake was born in Colombo, Sri Lanka. She is a talented Fashion Designer and Freelance Illustrator who has her own unique style. She has Illustrated more than 20 children's books including God's Great Garden.

You can contact her at: jayaminiattanayake@yahoo.com

Printed in the United States
By Bookmasters